In the Deep, Dark Forest

by Penny Dolan

2

Illustrated by David Lopez

W
FRANKLIN WATTS

First published in 2009 by
Franklin Watts
338 Euston Road
London
NW1 3BH

Franklin Watts Australia
Level 17/207 Kent Street
Sydney
NSW 2000

Text © Penny Dolan 2009
Illustration © David Lopez 2009

A CIP catalogue record for this book is available
from the British Library.

ISBN 978 0 7496 9183 7 (hbk)
ISBN 978 0 7496 9189 9 (pbk)

Series Editor: Jackie Hamley
Editor: Melanie Palmer
Series Advisor: Dr Barrie Wade
Series Designer: Peter Scoulding

Printed in China

Franklin Watts is a division of
Hachette Children's Books,
an Hachette UK company.
www.hachette.co.uk

In the deep, dark forest
was a deep, dark cave.

Into that forest rode
a knight so brave,

a knight on a horse

who had come from afar,

to the deep, dark forest
where the scary things are.

He rode past the trees
that stand and stare.

He rode past the thorns
that catch and tear.

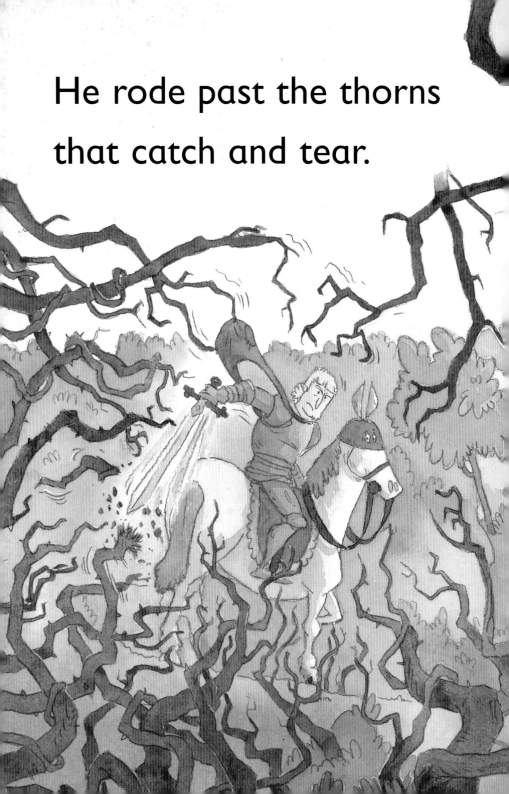

He crossed the old bridge
that had something under.

He passed the huge
waterfall that crashed
like thunder.

He passed by some animals out for a walk.

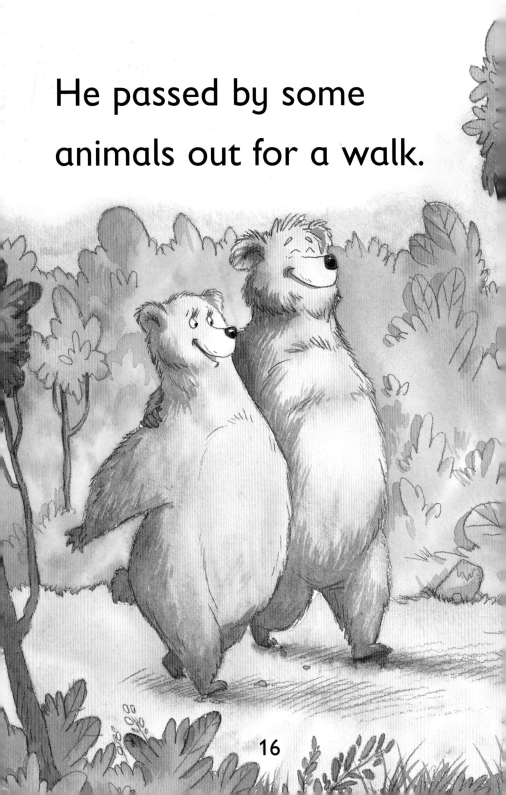

He rode through the stems
of a great beanstalk.

He rode till he saw
the deep, dark cave.

Then he tied up his horse,
that knight so brave.

And he went inside where
the dragon lay,

breathing its fire all
night and day.

He took off his sword
and undid his pack.

He put the marshmallows
all down in a stack.

And they let the marshmallows turn fluffy and brown,

as the blazing sun went down, down, down,

that dragon bold and the

knight so brave,

in the deep, dark forest,

in the deep, dark cave.

Puzzle 1

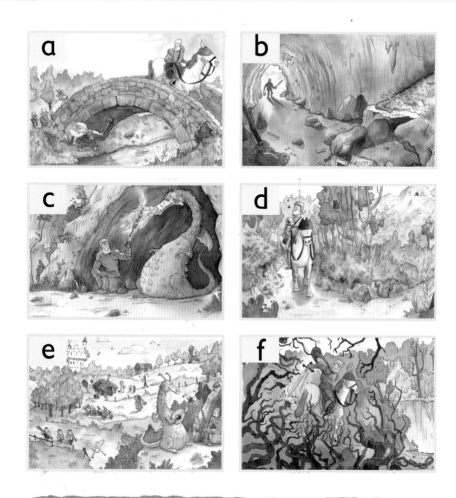

Put these pictures in the correct order.
Now retell the story in your own words.
Is there a lesson in the story?

Puzzle 2

knight	fright
bite	tree

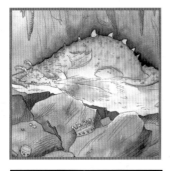

lair	flame
aim	tame

hide	inside
dark	sighed

Find the non-rhyming word in each word box. Can you think of some words to rhyme with the odd one out?

Answers

Puzzle 1

The correct order is: 1d, 2f, 3a, 4b, 5c, 6e

Puzzle 2

The odd words out are:

tree, lair, dark.

Look out for more Leapfrog Rhyme Time:

*hardback

For more Leapfrog books go to: www.franklinwatts.co.uk

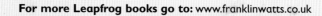